Pegasus Princesses
MIST'S MAZE

Pegasus Princesses

MIST'S MAZE

Emily Bliss

illustrated by **Sydney Hanson**

BLOOMSBURY
CHILDREN'S BOOKS
NEW YORK   LONDON   OXFORD   NEW DELHI   SYDNEY

BLOOMSBURY CHILDREN'S BOOKS
Bloomsbury Publishing Inc., part of Bloomsbury Publishing Plc
1385 Broadway, New York, NY 10018

BLOOMSBURY, BLOOMSBURY CHILDREN'S BOOKS, and the Diana logo
are trademarks of Bloomsbury Publishing Plc

First published in the United States of America in September 2021
by Bloomsbury Children's Books
www.bloomsbury.com

Text copyright © 2021 by Emily Bliss
Illustrations copyright © 2021 by Sydney Hanson

Bloomsbury books may be purchased for business or promotional use. For information on
bulk purchases please contact Macmillan Corporate and Premium Sales Department at
specialmarkets@macmillan.com

Library of Congress Cataloging-in-Publication Data
available upon request
ISBN 978-1-5476-0680-1 (paperback) • ISBN 978-1-5476-0681-8 (hardcover)
ISBN 978-1-5476-0682-5 (e-book)

Book design by Jessie Gang and John Candell
Typeset by Westchester Publishing Services
Printed and bound in the U.S.A.
2 4 6 8 10 9 7 5 3 (paperback)
2 4 6 8 10 9 7 5 3 1 (hardcover)

To find out more about our authors and books visit www.bloomsbury.com
and sign up for our newsletters.

For Phoenix and Lynx

Pegasus Princesses
MIST'S MAZE

Chapter One

In the library of Feather Palace, Princess Mist, a silver pegasus, flew slowly along the top shelf of books. Right behind her, Lucinda, a silver cat with wings, purred and practiced doing somersaults in the air.

"Where could it be?" Mist asked, hovering for a few seconds in front of a shelf and

then gliding forward to the next row of books. "This is where we keep the magic cookbooks. But I don't see it anywhere."

Lucinda twitched her tail. "How about if we play a guessing game while you're looking?" she asked. Then she flipped upside down and, with her paws sticking up toward the ceiling, flew in figure eights around Mist's hooves.

Mist laughed. "I promise I'll play a guessing game with you after I find this book. I've been wanting to host a cloud maze party for my sisters for months. But I can only do it if I know how to make—" Mist's eyes widened as she read the title *Magic Maze Potions* on the spine of a thick

red book. "Here it is!" Mist exclaimed. "Finally!" With her mouth, she pulled the book off the shelf.

Mist flew in an excited circle around a chandelier. She did a flip in the air. And then she swooped down to the floor and placed the book on a wooden desk next to a wing-shaped reading lamp with a rainbow flame. A second later, Lucinda landed with a thud on the desktop, right next to the book.

"Now can we play a guessing game?" Lucinda asked, looking up at Mist with large green eyes. "Please?"

"I promise we'll play one," Mist said. "But let's look up the recipe first."

Lucinda frowned with disappointment.

"How about if you help me turn the pages?" Mist asked, smiling at the cat.

Lucinda purred with delight and swished her tail. Then she used her paw to flip the book open to the table of contents. Mist and Lucinda leaned over the page. Mist began to read the names of the maze potions out loud: "Swirling Rainbow Maze Potion, page 3. Yodeling Corn Maze Potion, page 4. Underwater Coral Reef Maze Potion, page 5. Glowing Yarn Maze Potion, page 6. Blooming Flower Maze Potion, page 7. Glitter Garden Maze Potion, page 8." Then her eyes widened and she grinned. "Giant Floating Cloud Maze Party Potion, page 9," she read, flapping her wings with excitement

so her hooves lifted for a few seconds off the library's shiny black tile floor.

Lucinda purred and turned pages with her paw until the book lay open to page 9:

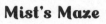
Giant Floating Cloud Maze Party Potion

YOU WILL NEED:

1 medium bottle

pollen from 4 ear-flowers

4 seconds of flowing water from a sky
     stream

1 human girl

DIRECTIONS:

Step One: In the potion bottle,
     collect the pollen from the
     ear-flowers.

Step Two: Immediately after
     completing step one, hold the bottle
     in a rapidly flowing sky stream for

four seconds. Note: Do not put a cap
on the bottle.

Step Three: Have a human girl cover the
bottle opening with her thumb and
shake the bottle four times.

Step Four: Pour out the contents of the
bottle in the sky at least 30 feet
above the highest treetop.

Step Five: Watch your cloud maze party
form right before your eyes.

Mist furrowed her brow. Lucinda
twitched her tail and cocked her head to
the side.

"I bet the hedgehogs in the Cloud Forest
would be happy to gather the ear-flower
pollen and the sky stream water for me,"

Mist said slowly. "But how are we going to find a human girl? There certainly aren't any in the Wing Realm."

"I'll find one for you, Princess Mist," Lucinda purred eagerly.

"Really?" Mist asked, eyes widening. "You will?"

"Absolutely," Lucinda said. "I'd love to help you."

Mist reared up and whinnied with delight. "Thank you," she said. "And one other thing. I would love to make friends with the human girl you find, and I bet my sisters would too. Will you try to find one that loves pegasuses?"

Lucinda nodded. "I promise I will," she said. Then she grinned hopefully. "Now

will you play a guessing game with me? Please?"

Mist laughed. "Of course," she said. "Thank you for waiting so patiently."

Lucinda grinned. "How about if I guess your favorite letter of the alphabet?"

"Okay," Mist said. "Don't forget that I love the sound of my name," she added with a wink.

Lucinda nodded. "I'll give myself three guesses," she said. "Is it A?"

Mist shook her head.

"Rats!" Lucinda said. She sighed and furrowed her brow. "How about X?"

Mist shook her head.

"Double rats!" Lucinda said. "I'm sure I'll get it this time. How about J?"

Mist shook her head again. "I'm afraid the answer is M. M for Mist."

"Triple rats!" Lucinda said. She twitched her tail. And then she smiled and shrugged. "I don't want to be a sore loser. Thanks for playing with me. There is nothing I love more than guessing games."

"Not even naps?" Mist asked, smiling.

"Well," Lucinda said, "I admit that maybe I do like naps just a little more than guessing games." She spread her wings and flew into the air. Hovering in front of Mist, she said, "And now I'll go find your human girl who loves pegasuses."

But suddenly Lucinda's eyelids began to droop. She yawned five times in a row. She dropped back down to the desktop

and, swaying back and forth as her eyes closed, she said, "I'll find your human girl as soon as I take a quick catnap." Then she curled up in a ball next to the potion book and began to snore.

Chapter Two

Clara Griffin was supposed to be cleaning her room. That was what her parents had asked her to do. And when she galloped into her bedroom—whinnying and wearing tin-foil pegasus wings and a pipe-cleaner tiara—she told herself that even pegasuses had to clean their stables sometimes.

She had gotten off to a good start. She

made her bed, straightening and tucking in her green pegasus sheets and pulling her matching bedspread up to the giant silver pegasus pillow she had sewn herself. She re-shelved all the books she and her younger sister, Miranda, had arranged in a circle on the floor to make a pegasus race track. She began putting away the clean clothes in the laundry basket on the floor next to her bureau. After she had put all her shirts in her shirt drawer, all her underwear in her underwear drawer, and all her socks in her sock drawer, she picked up her favorite dress—a green one with giant pockets and a picture of a silver pegasus on the front that she had made herself with fabric paints. She skipped over to her closet to

hang it up. And that was when she suddenly had an idea. The idea was much
more fun and much more interesting than
cleaning her room. What Clara wanted to
do, right then and there, was make a family
of pegasus princesses and build them a
magical palace in her closet.

Clara jumped up and down with excitement. She dropped the dress and bounded
over to her desk, which was covered in art
supplies from her last craft project—making
paper bag pegasus puppets with Miranda.
Clara collected a handful of Popsicle sticks,
two tubes of glitter glue, a roll of masking
tape, scissors, a glue stick, craft feathers,
and pink yarn. Then, sitting cross-legged
on her bedroom floor, she set about

making eight pegasus princesses. She pasted together the Popsicle sticks to build pegasus bodies. She taped on the feathers to give each pegasus wings. She tied on yarn to make manes and tails. And then, with glitter glue, she gave each pegasus a tiara. When she finished, she lined them up on the floor to dry.

Next, Clara bounded over to her closet. She gathered up her shoes and put them in a pile behind her. She pulled her dresses, shirts, skirts, and coats off their hangers and left them in a mound on her bed. For a few seconds, Clara surveyed the empty closet. She had plans to make pegasus bunk beds, a pegasus snack bar, and a pegasus bathtub. But what she wanted to build first

was something fun for the pegasus princesses to do. She considered a sandbox. Or a swing set. Or even a merry-go-round. Then she had an even better idea. What the pegasus princesses needed was a giant maze to fly through! And what she needed to make the maze were long sticks she could tie together with yarn and hang from the bar that spanned the top of her closet.

Clara bounded over to her bedroom door, ready to head outside to collect sticks. She reached for the doorknob. And then she noticed she was still wearing her pink pegasus pajamas, tin-foil wings, and pipe-cleaner tiara. Clara giggled. She took off her wings, her tiara, and her pajamas. And then she put on the green pegasus dress she had dropped on the floor, a pair of green-and-white-striped tights, and her lime-green canvas sneakers.

Clara burst out of her bedroom. She sprinted down the hall, hopped down the stairs two at a time, and danced into the living room. There her mother sat on the couch reading a novel while her father sat in an armchair doing a crossword puzzle with a red pen. Her sister, Miranda, lay on the floor studying a wildlife encyclopedia as she sketched a caterpillar in her nature journal.

"I'm going outside to get some sticks," Clara said, twirling in a circle. "I'll be right back."

"Have you already finished cleaning your room?" her mother asked.

"Um," Clara said. She had completely forgotten about cleaning her room. "I got started. And then—"

"Let me guess," her father said, his eyes twinkling. "You thought of a creative project while you were cleaning. And you absolutely had to start it right away."

Clara blushed. "Well," she said, "yes."

Her mother smiled. "Can you just promise you'll finish cleaning your room sometime this weekend?" she asked.

"I promise," Clara said.

Miranda looked up from her nature journal. "I'll help you clean your room later," she said. Miranda loved cleaning and organizing. In her room, all the books were arranged by topic on her shelves and then alphabetized by the author's last name—just like at the library. Inside her bureau drawers, her clothes were neatly folded and arranged in rainbow order. When she got bored, she did things like clean out the kitchen junk drawer or reorganize all the mittens, hats, and scarves in the closet by their front door.

"Thank you," Clara said, smiling at her sister.

"No problem," Miranda said. "I just want to finish drawing this caterpillar first."

Clara thought to herself that if she tried to draw a caterpillar, it would soon have a

dragon tail, a unicorn horn, and a five-story cocoon that doubled as a magic piano.

Clara skipped across the living room, through the kitchen, and out the back door. She hopped on one foot along the slate stones that led to the edge of the woods surrounding her house. She jogged down a trail that cut through a thick grove of tall pine trees, and she began collecting long thin sticks without too much bark.

But as she bent over to pick up a stick, she noticed something shiny ahead of her on the path. She skipped toward it, expecting it to be an interesting rock or a toy she and Miranda had accidentally left in the woods.

But Clara froze when she saw what it was: a shimmering silver feather.

For a moment, Clara stared at the feather. She tried to imagine what creature—maybe a magic silver bird—might have left it there. She took a few more steps toward the feather and kneeled next to it. As she leaned toward it, glittery light raced up and down the feather's spine, and she heard a soft humming noise. Clara sucked in her breath. And then she reached out her hand and picked it up.

As soon as her fingers touched the feather, glittery light swirled all around her. The humming noise grew louder. And then, right in front of her, there appeared a

light-green velvet armchair with two giant silver-feathered wings on its back. Sitting in the middle of the armchair, licking one of her paws and twitching her tail, was a silver cat. And, to Clara's astonishment, the cat also had wings.

For a few seconds, Clara watched the cat wash its face. And then Clara whispered, "Hello."

The cat looked up. She blinked her bright green eyes in surprise. And then she grinned. "Hello," she purred. "Are you, by any chance, a human girl?"

Clara could not believe her ears. The cat could talk! "Yes," she replied. "I am a human girl."

"Are you absolutely sure?" the cat asked.

Clara giggled. "Yes," she said.

"Well, that's a relief," the cat said. "I *have* met one before, but I'm having a little trouble identifying them lately. Yesterday I thought I had finally found a human girl, but she was actually a very large fairy with very small wings. We had to send her back to the Glitter Realm. And the day before that, I thought I had found a human girl, but it turned out she was a mermaid with two tails that I thought were legs. We had to send her back to the Aqua Realm." The cat shrugged.

Clara laughed. "I'm definitely not a fairy or a mermaid," she said.

The cat stood up on the chair and stretched. Then she jumped into the air and flew in a slow circle around Clara. "You don't happen to like pegasuses, do you?"

Clara's eyes widened. "I don't just like pegasuses," she said. "I *love* pegasuses."

The cat did an excited somersault. "You are exactly the girl I've been looking for," she purred. "Princess Mist will be very excited."

Clara raised her eyebrows. "Who is Princess Mist?" she asked.

"Princess Mist is one of the eight pegasus princesses who rule over the Wing Realm," Lucinda explained. Then, hovering in the air, she puffed out her chest and lifted her chin proudly. "And I am their royal pet cat, Lucinda."

"It's wonderful to meet you, Lucinda," Clara said. "My name is—"

"Wait! Please don't tell me!" Lucinda exclaimed, eyes wide with excitement. "Let me guess!"

Clara laughed. "Okay," she said.

"I just need three guesses," Lucinda purred. She flew up to Clara's face and touched her silvery-pink nose to Clara's nose. Clara giggled at the feeling of the cat's whiskers against her cheeks. "Is it Aballackanacka?" Lucinda asked, with her face still pressed up to Clara's.

"No," Clara said.

"Rats!" Lucinda said. She fluttered her wings to fly upward, and then, to Clara's surprise, she landed right on

Clara's head. "I'll get it this time. Is it Wallapopolous?"

"No," Clara said, smiling.

"Double rats!" Lucinda said. She flew down to the ground and sniffed Clara's lime-green sneakers. "Well, now I've got it. Is it Ringoctagon?"

"It's Clara," Clara said, laughing.

"Triple rats!" Lucinda said. She flattened her ears and twitched her tail. "Well, that was just bad luck. I would have gotten it on the next guess."

"Probably," Clara said politely.

"Thank you for playing with me," Lucinda said, weaving between Clara's ankles. "And now I'm wondering if you would be willing to come with me to the

Wing Realm. Princess Mist needs a human girl to help her make a cloud maze party potion."

"A cloud maze party potion?" Clara repeated. She could not think of anything that sounded more exciting than meeting a real pegasus princess—or eight!—and making a cloud maze party potion. "I would love to help," she said.

Lucinda purred with delight. "Wonderful. Go ahead and take a seat." She nodded at the green armchair.

Clara skipped over to the armchair. For a moment she looked at its silver-feathered wings, which began to slowly flap. She slipped the silver feather she had found in the woods into her pocket, and, with her

heart thundering in her chest, she sat down. Lucinda leaped onto Clara's lap. For a few seconds, Clara scratched behind Lucinda's ears and wings while Lucinda purred loudly. Then Lucinda curled up in a ball on Clara's lap and said, "Please take us to the Wing Realm."

The chair hopped forward into a bed of brown pine needles. It hopped again, skidding on some pinecones. It jumped onto a tree branch. For a moment it teetered back and forth before it leaped way up into the air and landed on the green tile roof of Clara's house. Clara gripped the arms of the chair as it spun around faster and faster. Then, still spinning, the chair sailed up into the sky. It climbed higher and higher and Clara, feeling dizzy, closed her eyes. Then all of a sudden the spinning stopped, and Clara felt the chair land.

Chapter Three

Clara opened her eyes. She sucked in her breath. She was sitting in the most fantastic room she had ever seen.

The walls were bright magenta. The floors were polished black marble. Painted portraits of pegasuses wearing tiaras covered the walls. Stone statues of pegasuses reared up on pedestals with outstretched wings. Pegasus fountains spouted rainbow water. Chandeliers made of gold feathers held candles that burned rainbow flames. Gauzy curtains billowed in the breeze over tall windows. In the center of the room, arranged in a half-circle, were eight large thrones: a silver throne with a swirl design; a turquoise throne with a water drop-let design; a white throne with a snowflake design; a green throne with a scissors, nee-dle, and thread design; a peach throne with a spiral design; a pink throne with a letter design; a black throne with a star design; and a lavender throne with an arrow design. Clara smiled when she also spotted a cat-sized velvet couch with a back shaped like a cat head. Below the triangular ears were two eyes made of green sequins. That one, Clara thought, had to be for Lucinda.

"Welcome to Feather Palace," Lucinda said, leaping off Clara's lap and strutting proudly in front of the thrones. "Do you like our new thrones? Princess Stitch made them for us last week."

"They're amazing," Clara said.

Lucinda leaped onto her silver cat couch and, in a loud voice, called out, "Princess Mist! I found one! This time, I really and truly found a human girl!"

Almost instantly Clara heard a clattering noise coming from down a hallway. The clattering grew louder and louder. And then a pegasus with a silver coat, a wavy silver mane, and a silver tail galloped into

the room. On her head she wore a tiara with a glittering swirl design made of gemstones. As soon as the pegasus saw Clara, a giant grin spread across her face. She reared up and whinnied with excitement, flapping her wings so that, for a moment, her shiny hooves lifted off the floor.

"Welcome to the Wing Realm," the

pegasus said in a warm, high voice. "I'm Princess Mist. I'm one of the eight pegasus princesses who live here in Feather Palace."

"It's wonderful to meet you," Clara said, feeling a little out of breath. "I'm Clara Griffin. I'm not a princess. I only have one sister. And I live in a house that doesn't have a name in Gardenview, New Jersey."

"Gardenview, New Jersey," Mist repeated in a whisper. "What a fascinating name. Someday I will have to visit there." She cocked her head to the side and smiled apologetically. "I don't want to be rude, but I just want to make absolutely and completely sure of something. Especially since we had a few, um, mix-ups over the past few days. You don't happen to be a large fairy with very, very small wings, do you?"

Clara laughed. "I'm not a fairy," she said.

"And your legs aren't actually two fish tails because you're really a mermaid, right?"

Clara laughed even harder. "I'm not a mermaid. I really am a human girl, just like Lucinda said," she replied.

Mist smiled with relief. "Well, in that case, Clara Griffin from Gardenview, New Jersey, I could not be any more excited that you are here."

"Well, Princess Mist from the Wing Realm, I don't think *I* could be any more excited that *I'm* here," Clara said.

"Did Lucinda happen to tell you why I was searching for a human girl?" Mist asked.

Clara glanced over at Lucinda, who was now lying on her cat couch busily licking one of her hind feet. "She said you needed my help to make a cloud maze party potion."

"Exactly," Mist said. "For months, I have dreamed of hosting a cloud maze party for my sisters and me in the sky above the Cloud Forest. I searched and searched for a magical cookbook with a cloud maze party potion recipe. I finally found one, and it turns out that to make the potion work, a human girl has to shake the bottle four times. Is there any chance you'd be willing to help me?"

"Absolutely," Clara said.

"Wonderful," Mist said. "And, on behalf of all eight pegasus princesses, I would like to invite you to our cloud maze party. We would be thrilled to have a human guest of honor."

"Thank you for the invitation," Clara said. Then she paused. "I'd love to come, but there's just one thing. If I stay here too long, my parents will start to worry about me."

"You're in luck," Mist said. "Time in the human world freezes while humans visit any of the magic realms. So, when you return to your house, your parents will think you've been gone only a few minutes."

"In that case, I would be thrilled to come to your cloud maze party. I've never been to one," Clara said.

"Neither have I," Mist said. "And I love doing new things."

"Me too," Clara agreed.

Mist grinned. "This is turning out to be the best day ever," she said. "In just a few minutes, we should leave for the Cloud Forest. The hedgehogs who live there have already made the potion. We'll go get it from them, you can shake it four times, we'll pour it out together in the sky, and then we can have our cloud maze party."

"That sounds like a great plan," Clara said. "I'm ready whenever you are."

Mist opened her mouth to respond, but just then Clara heard a clattering noise that was much louder than before. Seven more pegasus princesses burst into the room. Each was a different color, and each wore a tiara.

As soon as the pegasuses saw Clara, they stopped galloping. For a few seconds, they stared hard at Clara. She couldn't be sure, but it seemed like they were looking to see if there were tiny wings on her back or if her legs were actually fish tails. Then they all turned to Mist with excited, hopeful faces.

"Allow me to introduce you to my new

human friend, Clara Griffin, from Garden-view, New Jersey," Mist said.

All eight pegasus princesses reared up and whinnied with excitement. They flapped their wings and flew in excited circles. After a few seconds of celebration, they each landed on a throne that was the same color as their coat.

"Welcome to Feather Palace," said a turquoise pegasus wearing a tiara with a water droplet design. "I'm Princess Aqua. We're so glad you're here. Feel free to have a seat." She nodded toward the green winged armchair Clara and Lucinda had flown to Feather Palace.

"Thank you, but honestly I think I'm a little too excited to sit down," Clara said, giggling and hopping from one foot to the other.

"Well then, feel free to stand and hop," said a pink pegasus. She wore a tiara with a jumble of gemstone letters. "I'm Princess Rosetta, but you can call me Rosie."

"I think you must be the only creature in the Wing Realm right now without wings," said a peach pegasus wearing a tiara with gemstones arranged in spirals. She smiled and winked. "I'm Princess Flip."

"We couldn't be more pleased you're here," a black pegasus said, smiling warmly. "I'm Princess Star." Her tiara had gemstone stars, moons, and planets.

"I'm Princess Stitch," said a green

pegasus wearing a tiara with a scissors, needle, and thread design. "We are thrilled to have a human friend."

"I'm Princess Dash," a lavender pegasus said. "It's so nice to meet you." Her tiara had a gemstone arrow design.

"And I'm Princess Snow," a white pegasus wearing a tiara with a gemstone snowflake design said. "Welcome!"

"It's amazing to meet all of you," Clara said. "Thank you for inviting me here. I can't wait to help with the cloud maze party potion."

Mist, Aqua, Snow, Stitch, Rosie, Flip, Star, and Dash all grinned. Then Mist looked at Clara with twinkling eyes and said, "Are you ready to come with me to the Cloud Forest?"

"Absolutely," Clara said.

Mist leaped off her throne, trotted over to Clara, and kneeled. "Climb on up," she said.

Clara sucked in her breath. She was about to ride a pegasus! She swung her leg over Mist's silver back and held on to Mist's shiny mane, which felt cool and silky. Mist stood up, turned her head to the side, and smiled at Clara. "I've never had a passenger before," she said.

"I've never ridden a pegasus before," Clara said.

They both laughed.

Mist turned to Lucinda. "Did you want to come with us to the Cloud Forest?" she asked.

Lucinda finished licking her paw and looked up. "I'll meet you there as soon as I play a guessing game with Princess Snow," she purred. "I'm going to try to guess her favorite season in four tries. I think my first guess will be summer."

Clara kept herself from giggling. She didn't want to hurt Lucinda's feelings.

The pegasus princesses all looked at each other, and Clara could tell they were trying not to giggle, too.

"That sounds good, Lucinda," Mist said. "We'll see you soon." Then she looked at her sisters. "Want to meet above the

Cloud Forest in about an hour? I think Clara and I will be all ready by then."

"Sounds great," Aqua said.

"I can't wait," Star and Snow said at exactly the same time.

"See you there," Rosie said.

Flip and Dash nodded and swished their tails.

"I'll come a little early just in case you need any help with the potion," Stitch said.

"Thanks, Stitch," Mist said. Then she turned and trotted toward the palace's double front doors. When she was a few feet in front of them, the doors swung open. Clara peered outside, expecting to see a palace garden with fountains, rose bushes, and more pegasus statues. But instead she

saw blue sky, clouds, and treetops. The palace was floating in the air!

"Hold on tight!" Mist said.

Clara tightened her grip on Mist's mane as the silver pegasus leaped forward and flew out the palace doors.

Chapter Four

As Mist soared into the sky, Clara turned her head and gazed back at Feather Palace. The castle, which looked like two enormous silver wings surrounded by towers and turrets, sparkled in the sun. "Your palace is beautiful," Clara said.

"Thank you," Mist said, flying higher

and higher. "I can't wait to show you the Cloud Forest. I think it's even more beautiful than Feather Palace. It's just a little further up this way."

"I can't wait to see it," Clara said.

Mist paused. And then she said, "Can I ask you something I've been wondering about?"

"Of course," Clara said.

"Do you have any magic powers?" Mist asked.

"I pretend I have magic powers all the time," Clara said. "And my parents would say my magic power is to make messes when I do creative projects. But the truth is, I'm not magic at all."

"Interesting," Mist said. "Do any of the humans in Gardenview, New Jersey, have magic powers?"

"No," Clara said, laughing. "Humans are just not magic." She paused. "Do you have any magic powers?"

Mist turned her head back toward Clara. "I'll show you," she said in a playful voice. "Though honestly, it's not very interesting."

The swirl design on Mist's tiara sparkled. And then, all of a sudden, Mist disappeared. Except Clara could still feel Mist's back under her. She could still feel Mist's mane in her hands. She could even still occasionally feel a feather from Mist's wings brushing against her leg. "Are you still here?" Clara asked, feeling nervous.

"I sure am," Mist said. And then, suddenly, Mist reappeared. "My magic power is just to turn invisible." She sighed and added, "It's nothing fancy or special."

"I think being able to turn invisible is an amazing magic power," Clara said.

"Really?" Mist asked, sounding surprised.

"Yes," Clara said. "I would love to be able to make myself invisible."

"Well, thank you," Mist said, sounding pleased. "Honestly, sometimes I feel like all my sisters' magic powers are better than mine. Aqua can breathe underwater and make bubbles. Snow can freeze things and create snow. Stitch can magically sew, knit, or crochet almost anything. Rosie can

speak and understand any language. Flip can do a magic somersault and then turn into any animal. Star can magically feel, see, hear, and smell things no one else can. Dash can instantly transport herself anywhere within the Wing Realm. Being able to turn invisible just seems so boring." Mist sighed.

"I really do think being able to turn invisible is a wonderful magic power," Clara said. "But I also completely understand how you feel when you compare yourself to your sisters. I feel jealous of my sister, Miranda, all the time. I feel jealous of how curly her hair is and how fast she can run. And when she learned to pump on a swing before I did, even though I'm older than she is, I felt so jealous I could hardly stand it."

"I know exactly what you mean," Mist said. "Snow is younger than I am, and she learned to fly before I did. I did not like that one bit."

"Do you know what my mother says when my sister and I feel jealous of each other?" Clara said, smiling. "She says, 'Comparison is the thief of joy.' It's a little annoying when she says it. But I have to admit it's true."

Mist laughed. "I definitely do not feel joy when I'm comparing myself to my sisters. So your mother is probably right," she said.

"I know I only just met you, but I want

you to know I like you exactly the way you are. I wouldn't want you to have a different magical power," Clara said.

"Thank you," Mist said. "I can already tell you're going to be a wonderful friend. And I don't think that just because you're human and you can help me make my potion. I think that because you're kind. After talking to you, I'm even starting to feel proud of being able to turn invisible."

"I can tell you're going to be a wonderful friend too," Clara said. "And that's not just because you're a pegasus. You're *also* kind, and that is the most important way for a friend to be."

Mist turned toward Clara and smiled.

Then she faced forward. "Do you see those clouds up ahead? That's the Cloud Forest. We're almost there. This is going to be so much fun."

Clara looked off in the distance and saw the edge of what looked like a thick blanket of silvery-pink clouds. As they flew closer and closer, Clara saw a stone wall a few feet from the edge of the cloud floor. And in the wall was a wooden door with a sign above it that said, in swirly silver writing, *Welcome to the Cloud Forest.*

Mist flew up to the door. And then, to Clara's astonishment, she landed right on the pink clouds. "Would you like to get down?" she asked.

"Can I really walk on the clouds?" Clara asked.

"These are special magic clouds," Mist said. "I promise you won't fall through them. Though I don't usually walk on them."

"What do you do instead?" Clara asked.

"You'll see," Mist said in a playful voice as she kneeled.

Clara slid off her back. Under her feet, the clouds felt spongy and springy—just like a trampoline. Clara bent her knees, about to jump. She glanced over at Mist, who was also bending her knees, about to jump. They locked eyes and grinned at each other. And then, at exactly the same time, they jumped high into the air. "Whee!" Clara called out. She landed and jumped again. And again. And then again.

"One of the best things about the Cloud Forest is you can jump along all the paths instead of walking or flying," Mist said, jumping up and somersaulting in the air. "So," she continued, bouncing from side to side, "are you ready to see the Cloud Forest and get the potion from the hedgehogs?"

"Yes," Clara said.

"Jump up to the gate and close your eyes," Mist said. "I want to surprise you."

Clara hopped over to the door and shut her eyes. She held her breath as she heard the door creak open. Then, Mist said, "Take six jumps forward."

Clara jumped six times. She heard the

gate swing closed behind her. "Now you can look," Mist said.

Clara opened her eyes. She stood at the edge of a forest—but it was unlike any forest she had ever seen. All the trees were completely silver, with shimmering silver trunks, silver leaves, silver pine needles, and silver pinecones. And everywhere, Clara could see silvery-pink mist. Wide ribbons of mist spiraled up tree trunks. Thin threads of mist slid along tree branches. Tangled balls of mist drifted slowly in the air.

"This is an incredible place," Clara said.

"I had a feeling you'd like it," Mist said. "This path leads right to the hedgehogs'

tree. And on the way, I can show you something really neat."

Mist began to jump along a pink cloud path that cut through a thick grove of silver cedar trees. Clara jumped alongside her, closing her eyes for a moment to breathe in the cedar smell.

The path wound through patches of silver ferns blanketed in a thin layer of pink mist, silver willow trees wrapped in pink mist ribbons, and giant rocks covered in glittery, silver moss. Just before the path turned sharply to the left, Mist stopped jumping and looked at Clara. She whispered, "What I want to show you is just ahead. Follow me for a moment and be as quiet as possible."

Mist crept slowly off the path and stood behind a thick, silver tree trunk. Clara tip-toed right behind her. "If you look this way," Mist said, nodding toward a clearing on the other side of the tree, "you can see the two-lips and the ear-flower tree."

Clara peered over a bush. Sure enough, Clara saw a tall thin tree with large yellowy-silver flowers that looked just like pegasus ears. Below the tree was a patch of reddish-silver flowers shaped like giant mouths. "Do you see the ear-flowers and the two-lips?" Mist whispered.

"Yes," Clara whispered.

"Now, watch this," Mist whispered. "Come with me." They crept back to the path and walked silently along it as it passed

right in front of the ear-flower tree and the two-lips. Immediately, the two-lips turned their flowers toward Clara and Mist. The mouth-shaped flowers grinned. And then they began to sing, "Hello! Hello! Hello!"

As soon as the two-lips began to sing, the ear-flowers rolled up and curled into tight balls.

"That's amazing," Clara said.

Mist nodded. "The only way to see the ear-flowers is to hide where the two-lips don't notice you and sneak a peek. They're some of my favorite Cloud Forest plants."

"Thanks so much for showing me," Clara said.

"My pleasure," Mist said. "So, shall we go get the potion from the hedgehogs now?"

"That sounds great," Clara said. She and Mist jumped along a path as it crossed a field of long silver grass and snaked up a hillside. Ribbons and balls of mist drifted through the air and shimmered in the sunshine. And then Clara and Mist came to an enormous silver tree covered in threads and ribbons of mist. On each of the branches hung a purple hammock. And in each hammock was a sleeping purple animal with shiny violet wings, a pointy nose, purple bristles, and a tiny tail.

"Those are the hedgehogs," Mist said. "They're awake all night, and they sleep here all day."

Mist walked over to a hammock on the

lowest branch. In a soft voice, she whispered, "Hannah?"

The hedgehog stirred and made a snoring noise.

"Hannah? It's Princess Mist. I'm here to get the potion. I finally found a human girl," Mist whispered again, but this time a little louder.

Hannah sat up in her hammock. She opened one bright purple eye and then the other. She yawned and smiled. "The potion is all ready for you. I followed the recipe exactly and left it on the patch of moss on the other side of our tree."

"Thank you so much," Mist said. "I really appreciate it."

"It was a lot of fun to help you," Hannah said, yawning. "And now, I'd really better go back to sleep. We're having a hedgehog dance party tonight in the ballroom under our tree, and I don't want to be tired and cranky the whole time."

"Of course," Mist said, smiling. "Sleep well, and thanks again."

Hannah yawned. She curled up in a ball in her hammock and began to snore.

"Let's go get the potion," Mist said. She and Clara walked together around the tree, careful not to bump into any of the hedgehogs' hammocks. Sure enough, on a patch of silver moss stood a glass bottle full of a swirling, glittery yellow liquid.

Mist looked at Clara with wide, excited eyes. "Want to go pick it up?" she asked.

"Yes!" Clara said.

But before Clara could walk over to the bottle, a voice purred, "Wait for me! Princess Mist! Clara! Wait!"

Clara giggled. She and Mist turned around. There was Lucinda, grinning and bouncing along the path. "Sorry I'm late," she said, rubbing against Clara's and Mist's ankles. "My guessing game with Princess Snow took much longer than I expected. She told me I could have as many guesses as I wanted. I guessed Summer and then Spring and then Fall. Then I guessed Sprummer, which is my name for the time right between Spring and Summer. And then I guessed Sull, which is my name for the time right between

Summer and Fall. Finally, I guessed the right answer."

"Was it winter?" Clara asked.

"How did you know?" Lucinda asked, looking shocked.

"Just a lucky guess," Clara said gently.

Lucinda shrugged. Then she noticed the potion bottle. She twitched her tail and bounded over to it. She sniffed the top. She crouched in front of it and watched the glittery liquid swirl. She walked in three excited circles around it. And then, all of a sudden, she yawned five times in a row. Her eyelids fluttered. She swayed back and forth. "I feel an emergency catnap coming on," she said, as her eyelids drooped. "Don't

mind me." And then, as she curled up at the bottom of the tree, her tail knocked over the bottle of cloud maze potion. Clara rushed forward to pick up the bottle. But before she could turn it upright, all of the potion had spilled out into a puddle on the moss.

Chapter Five

"Oh no!" Mist gasped, watching as the moss absorbed more and more of the potion.

"I'm sorry I couldn't get to the bottle in time," Clara said. She felt her heart sink.

"You don't need to apologize," Mist said, as tears formed in her eyes. "It's not your fault." She paused. "It's not even really

Lucinda's fault. She didn't do it on purpose."

Clara looked at her new pegasus friend and said, "Would it be okay if I gave you a hug?"

Mist nodded. Clara wrapped her arms around Mist's shoulders and said, "I bet you feel really disappointed."

"What will we do?" Mist sniffled as tears streamed down her face. "I guess we'll just have to cancel the cloud maze party."

Clara took a step back and kept a hand on Mist to comfort her. "Couldn't we just make another bottle of potion now?" Clara asked. "I'd be glad to help in any way I can."

Mist looked down at her hooves and

shook her head. "I don't think so. The potion sounds easy to make because it only has two ingredients, ear-flower pollen and sky-stream water. The water would be easy to get. There's a sky stream just a little further down this path. But I can't think of any way for either of us to get the ear-flower pollen. The ear-flowers have to be open to collect the pollen. But if we get anywhere near them, the two-lips will start singing and the ear-flowers will close."

"How did Hannah the hedgehog get the pollen?" Clara asked.

"The two-lips close their flowers when it's dark," Mist said. "Hannah collected the pollen in the middle of the night."

Clara nodded. "Could you make

yourself invisible, so the two-lips don't see you, and collect the pollen?" she asked.

"My magic power would actually be useful for once if I could do that," Mist said, laughing through her tears. "The problem is my hooves. I could probably hold the potion bottle in my mouth, but there's no way I could get the pollen from the flowers without fingers."

Clara looked down at Mist's shiny silver hooves. She could see that Mist was right.

Just then, Clara turned and saw a green blur jumping toward them along the path in the distance. Soon Clara could make out two green wings, a green mane, and a long green tail. It was Stitch bounding toward them.

"Hello," Stitch sang out, grinning. But then she saw Mist's face. "What's wrong?" Stitch asked.

"Look," Mist said, nodding toward the sleeping Lucinda and the overturned bottle.

"Oh dear," Stitch said. "I think I know exactly what happened." Tears welled up in Stitch's eyes. "I guess we'll have to cancel the cloud maze party. Should I fly back to Feather Palace and tell the others not to meet us here?"

Mist looked at Clara. "You don't have any other ideas for how we could make more cloud maze party potion, do you? I wish I could somehow make you turn invisible along with me. Then you could ride on

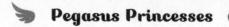

my back and collect the pollen. But," she sighed, "that's not possible."

Clara paused. "Let me think for just a minute longer," she said. She looked at the swirls on Mist's tiara and the scissors, needle, and thread design on Stitch's tiara. She watched several balls of tangled mist float between the branches of the hedgehogs' tree. And then she suddenly had an idea.

Clara smiled and hopped up and down with excitement. "I may not be able to be invisible with you," she said, "but what you said just made me think of a plan to get the ear-flower pollen right now, during the day."

"I will do anything to help," Mist said.

"Me too," Stitch said, nodding.

"I'm not completely sure it will work," Clara said. "But we won't know unless we try." She looked at Stitch. "Mist told me your magic power is that you can sew, knit, or crochet almost anything. Do you think you could use threads of mist to knit me a mist costume?"

Stitch cocked her head to the side. She furrowed her brow in confusion. "But Princess Mist isn't pink, and she isn't actually made of mist," Stitch said. "Do you want me to go get some silver, furry fabric and some feathers to make you a pegasus costume?"

Clara laughed and shook her head.

"Thank you for the offer," she said. "What I meant is I want a costume that will make me look like a cloud of mist."

Stitch's eyes widened and she grinned. "Well, there is nothing I love more than a craft challenge. I've never knitted with threads of mist. It may not work. But I'll give it my best shot."

Stitch looked for a moment at all the threads of mist spiraling around the trunk and sliding along the branches of the hedgehogs' tree. She took a long deep breath. Then, the scissors, needle, and thread design on her tiara sparkled. In the air in front of them appeared a gold tape measure. For a moment it spun in the air. Then, it danced over to Clara, and it

began measuring her. Clara giggled at the tickling feeling of the tape measure under her armpits, on the back of her head, and along her legs.

The tape measure vanished, and Stitch's tiara sparkled again. Two giant gold knitting needles appeared in front of them and twirled in the air. As the needles spun, the strands of mist peeled off the hedgehogs' tree and drifted toward each other until they formed one long thread. Golden light swirled around the mist as it rolled into a large ball. The knitting needles spun faster and faster, and then they began to knit the mist so quickly that they looked like a blur of gold. After just a few seconds, a pink, shimmering dress with long, loose sleeves and a large hood hung in the air. The knitting needles spun for a second and then vanished.

"Wow," Clara whispered, staring at the mist costume as it fluttered in the breeze.

"That was easier than I thought it would be," Stitch said, looking pleased. "Do you want to try it on?"

"Yes please," Clara said.

"Lift up your arms," Stitch said with an excited smile.

Clara raised her arms. Stitch's tiara sparkled for a moment, and then the mist costume floated to Clara and drifted downward, right over her head.

The costume felt cool, silky, and light. The sleeves hung over her hands, the

bottom covered her feet, and the hood was so big it flopped down over her face. Clara couldn't see perfectly through the hood, but she could definitely see well enough. She sat down and curled up in a ball. "Do I look like a mist cloud?" she asked.

"You look exactly like a mist cloud," Mist and Stitch said at exactly the same time.

"Perfect," Clara said. She stood up and jumped over to the potion bottle, which still lay on its side next to a snoring Lucinda. Clara picked it up and looked at Mist. "Might I get onto your back?" she asked.

"Of course," Mist said. She kneeled, and Clara, careful not to rip her costume or drop the bottle, climbed between Mist's wings.

"This is when your magic power will be extremely useful," Clara said to Mist. "If you make yourself invisible and fly with me on your back over to the ear-flower tree, I'm hoping the two-lips will just think I'm a cloud of mist drifting by and they won't start singing. If you hover by the ear-flowers for a few seconds, I'll quickly collect the pollen."

"That is an amazing plan," Mist said. "Let's do it!" The swirl design on Mist's tiara sparkled and, in an instant, she disappeared.

"Good luck," Stitch said. "I'm crossing my hooves for you." She winked and put

one shiny green front hoof over the other. "I'll meet you at the sky stream in just a few minutes."

"See you soon," Mist said, flying up into the air and back toward the ear-flowers and the two-lips. When they could see the ear-flower tree in the distance, Mist slowed down to a gentle drift. Slowly they drew closer and closer, until they were flying right over the two-lips. Clara sucked in her breath as the two-lips turned their mouth-shaped flowers upward. And then she exhaled with relief when they didn't start singing.

Mist hovered next to an ear-flower tree branch.

"Are you close enough to collect some pollen?" she whispered.

"Yes," Clara whispered. "How much do I need?"

"The recipe said to get pollen from four ear-flowers," Mist whispered.

Moving her arms and hands slowly, so they would look like drifting ribbons of mist, Clara used her fingers to pinch yellowy-silver dust from inside an ear-flower. She dropped the pollen into the potion bottle and reached toward a second ear-flower. Again, she pinched out the pollen and dropped it into the bottle. Then, she collected pollen from a third and then a fourth flower.

"I'm all finished," Clara whispered excitedly.

"Hooray," Mist sang out, and she reappeared.

The two-lips immediately began to sing. The ear-flowers curled up into tight balls. And Mist soared up into the sky. Clara pushed the hood off her face and head and called out, "We did it!"

Chapter Six

ist flew in an excited circle above the treetops. "That was an amazing plan," she said. "Thank you so much for thinking of it and for collecting the pollen."

"You're welcome," Clara said. "I am so very glad to help."

Mist swooped downward, wove around

some silver willow trees, and landed on the bank of a stream, right next to Stitch. "Did it work?" Stitch asked, hopping from side to side.

"It sure did," Clara said, holding up the bottle with the pollen in the bottom.

Stitch reared up and whinnied with excitement as Mist kneeled and Clara slid off her back.

"The next step is to collect four seconds' worth of sky-stream water," Mist said. She looked at Clara. "Would you be willing to do it? I think it's probably easier with hands than hooves."

"Absolutely," Clara said. She walked over to the edge of the silvery-blue water. She dipped the bottle into the current and counted slowly to four. Then she pulled the bottle out of the stream.

Clara, Mist, and Stitch all stared at the potion. Glittery yellow liquid swirled and bubbled. The bottle felt warm in Clara's hands.

Mist smiled excitedly at Clara and said, "Now, as our human guest of honor, please cover the top of the bottle with your thumb and shake it four times."

Clara sucked in her breath. She put her thumb over the top. And then she shook the bottle four times. The potion began to shine and shimmer. It turned scarlet, then bright orange, fluorescent yellow, lime green, robin's-egg blue, and finally a glittery swirling purple.

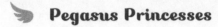

"Wow," Stitch whispered.

"Let's go make the cloud maze party!" Mist said, and she kneeled so Clara could climb onto her back. Clara held onto the potion and Mist's mane as Mist and Stitch flew high up into the sky. When they were far from the treetops, the two pegasus princesses looked at each other. And then Mist said, "Go ahead and pour it out."

Clara lifted the bottle of warm purple bubbling potion. She held her breath. Then she turned the bottle upside down.

The purple potion floated in the air for a few seconds. The liquid bubbled and foamed until it looked like a purple fluffy ball. The ball grew and grew, until it was the size of Clara's bedroom and then the

size of Clara's house. A heart-shaped opening appeared on the ball with a sign that read, in glittery purple writing, CLOUD MAZE PARTY ENTRANCE.

"We did it!" Mist said, laughing with joy. "We saved the cloud maze party! Thank you so much to both of you for all your help."

"We all worked together," Clara said. "We couldn't have done it without both of your amazing and unique magic powers." She winked at Mist. And Mist winked back.

Just then, Clara heard the sound of wings flapping. She looked behind her as Aqua, Snow, Rosie, Flip, Star, and Dash flew right up to Clara, Mist, and Stitch.

"Wow," Star said, "I can't wait to go inside."

"This looks amazing," Flip said.

"It looks incredible," Rosie said.

"I promise not to cheat by using my magic to dash to the center," Dash said with a playful grin.

"It's even bigger than I imagined," Snow said.

"We're so glad you're joining us," Aqua said, looking at Clara.

"I'm so glad I'm here," Clara replied.

"Should one of us go wake up Lucinda?" Stitch asked. "She'll be so disappointed if she doesn't get to join us."

But before anyone could respond, a voice purred, "Wait! Wait for me!"

Clara turned, and there was Lucinda zooming toward them.

"You're here just in time," Mist said, smiling at the silver cat.

"Sorry about that emergency catnap," Lucinda said. "I hope it didn't cause any trouble."

Clara, Mist, and Stitch all looked at each other and giggled.

Then Mist said, "Thank you so much to all of you for coming. At the count of three, let's all fly into the cloud maze. The goal is to get to the center, where we'll have a party. But just one thing. Would it be okay with all of you if we agreed that it's not a race to see who can get to the center first?"

Aqua, Snow, Dash, Star, Flip, Rosie, Stitch, Clara, and Lucinda all nodded.

"Good thinking," Aqua said. "It doesn't matter who's first or last."

"Let's just have fun," Snow said.

"Great," Mist said. "Let's go! One. Two. Three!"

Mist, with Clara on her back, flew into the cloud maze with Lucinda and the other seven pegasus princesses right behind her. They entered a small room made entirely of purple clouds with the entrances to six different tunnels. Aqua paused and then disappeared into a tunnel to the right. Flip and Rosie turned left to dive down a tunnel slide. Dash flew into a tunnel that jutted

upward and to the right. Star barreled down a tunnel that went straight down. Stitch flew into a tunnel to the right, and Lucinda followed her. "Which way shall we go?" Mist asked Clara.

"Let's go straight up," Clara suggested.

"Sounds good," Mist said, and she flew directly upward until they came to another tiny room with six more tunnel entrances. "Want to take turns choosing which way we go?" Mist asked.

"That's a great idea," Clara said. "Now it's your turn."

"Let's see where this slide goes," Mist said, looking down and to the left. She turned and jumped onto the soft cloud slide. "Whee!" Clara shrieked as they curved down and around and landed in a place with five more tunnel entrances.

"How about this way," Clara said, pointing toward a tunnel to her right.

"Sure thing," Mist said, and she flew through the tunnel.

Mist and Clara took turns choosing tunnels until they took a slide that landed in a big purple room. Balloons and streamers covered the ceiling. Music played. On a table in the center of the room were heart-shaped purple cupcakes and a heart-shaped trough of bubbly purple juice. Stitch, Aqua, and Lucinda were already there, dancing to the music. Flip and Rosie arrived on two different slides at the same time. They laughed, galloped over to the cupcakes,

and started eating. Snow, Dash, and Star landed in the room from another slide and rushed to drink from the trough.

"I'm getting hungry," Mist said, kneeling as Clara slid off her back. "Let's have cupcakes."

"Okay," Clara said, wondering what the cupcakes would taste like.

Mist trotted over to the tray and ate a cupcake in one giant gulp. Clara giggled and picked one up in her hand. She felt a little nervous but took a bite. And then she smiled. The cupcake tasted like a combination of mint, chocolate, and raspberries. And while it tasted good, Clara realized she was hungry for human food—particularly for healthy human

food. She also realized that while she had had an amazing time with the pegasus princesses, she missed Miranda and her parents.

Clara leaned over to Mist and said, "I have had such an amazing time here. But I think I'm ready to go home now."

Mist nodded. "I completely understand. Thank you so much for being our guest. I'm grateful to have made friends with you. You made me realize that I have a pretty great magical power. And that even though it's normal to feel jealous of my sisters, I am also happy that I am me."

"I'm so glad that we're friends," Clara said. "This visit has been the most fun I've ever had."

"We would love for you to come back anytime," Aqua said.

Stitch nodded. "Absolutely," she said.

Mist looked at Clara and smiled. "Do you still have the feather you found in the woods? The one Lucinda left for you?"

Clara pushed her hand in her dress pocket. Sure enough, the feather was still there. "I have it," she said. "Do you need it back?"

Mist shook her head. "That feather is our gift to you," she said. "If you run out into the woods while you're holding it, a flying chair will appear. Climb onto the chair and ask it to take you to Feather Palace. And it will take you directly to the front hall of our castle."

"Thank you so much," Clara said.

"If we ever want to invite you to the Wing Realm for a special occasion, the feather will shimmer and make a humming noise," Aqua said.

Clara grinned. "That sounds perfect," she said. "I'll keep it in a special place in my bedroom."

"You can also use the feather to go home," Mist said. "Whenever you're ready to leave the Wing Realm, hold it in your hands and say, 'Take me home, please.'"

Clara nodded. "I'm ready to go. Thank you again. And goodbye for now. I'll see you soon."

"Goodbye!" all eight pegasus princesses said at once.

"Come back soon!" Aqua said.

"You really are always welcome," Snow said.

Lucinda purred and rubbed against Clara's ankles.

Clara held up the feather. "Take me home, please," she said.

There was a flash of light. Clara felt herself flying up into the air, spinning faster and faster. Everything went pitch black. And suddenly she found herself sitting in the woods, right next to the pile of sticks she had collected. For a few seconds, she sat holding the feather and grinning, her heart beating fast in her chest. She stood up and noticed something soft and round in her dress pocket. She slid her hand into her pocket and pulled out a small ball of pink silky mist. Clara grinned and squeezed the mist. She knew exactly what she would do with it: she would use it to tie the sticks together to make the pegasus maze in her closet. Clara returned the feather and the ball of mist to her pocket. She picked up the sticks. And then she ran along the path, back toward her house, with her arms outstretched and flapping like wings.

Don't miss our next high-flying adventure!

Turn the page for a sneak peek ...

he front hall of Feather Palace
looked just the way Clara
remembered it from her first
visit. Gauzy curtains fluttered in the breeze
over feather-shaped windows. Portraits of
the eight pegasus princesses and Lucinda
hung on magenta walls. Light danced and
glittered on the shiny black marble floors.
On stone pedestals, pegasus statues reared

up, wings outstretched. Pegasus fountains spouted rainbow water. Eight empty thrones—each with a color and design that matched one of the pegasus princesses—were arranged in a horseshoe shape in the center of the room. Clara grinned when she saw that Lucinda's small silver sofa, with its back shaped like a cat head, was pushed right next to Aqua's teal throne.

At first Clara thought she was alone in the front hall. But then she heard a voice above her call out, "At the count of three, start kicking." Clara looked up. Just below the front hall's vaulted ceiling, all eight pegasus princesses were flying in a giant circle. They were all wearing large teal flippers strapped to their hooves. And they

were so immersed in their swimming lesson they didn't notice Clara had arrived.

Aqua swished her tail and said, "One. Two. Three. Kick!"

The pegasus princesses began to kick their front and back legs as they flew.

"Those kicks look great," Aqua said. "Now, start paddling with your wings like this." She swept her wings from front to back.

Mist, Stitch, Rosie, Star, and Dash all began to paddle their wings as they kicked. But Snow jabbed a flipper into her wing, stopped kicking, and then flew sideways as she tried to paddle. Flip swept her wings from back to front and bolted backward, flailing her legs in every direction. After a few seconds, Flip and Snow crashed into each other.

"Oops! Sorry!" Flip said to Snow.

"That was at least half my fault," Snow said, sighing. "I'm sorry too."

Flip groaned in frustration. "Every time I try to paddle, it's a disaster," she said.

Snow shook her head and snorted. "I feel so frustrated," she said. "I need to take a break from this swimming lesson."

"Wait!" Aqua called out, hurrying over to Flip and Snow. "You can't give up now. I know you can learn to swim. You just need to keep trying."

Flip and Snow glared at Aqua.

"I'm trying my hardest," Snow said. "Right now, it's just not working."

"I'm trying my hardest too," Flip said. "And I'm getting so frustrated that I need to do something else for a little while. Otherwise, I feel like I might explode!"

Aqua's face looked panicked. "I know you're both trying your hardest. And I really appreciate it. But you can't quit now. The Merthday Splash is *this afternoon*. If you can't swim by the time the celebration begins, the whole thing will be ruined," she said. "Could you please try again? I really think you've almost got it."

Flip groaned and flared her nostrils. "I promise I will keep trying," she said. "But not right now."

Snow nodded. "I'm willing to try swimming one more time before the Merthday

Splash," she said. "But first I'm taking a break with Flip."

Aqua bit her lip and flattened her ears with worry as Flip and Snow dived down to their thrones. They snorted and frowned as they pushed off their flippers and shoved them onto the floor. And then, as they looked back up at each other, they both noticed Clara sitting in the green armchair opposite them. Flip and Snow's eyes widened in surprise. Their frowns turned into enormous grins. And then they both leaped off their thrones and galloped over to Clara.

Emily Bliss, also the author of the Unicorn Princesses series, lives with her winged cat in a house surrounded by woods. From her living room window, she can see silver feathers and green flying armchairs. Like Clara Griffin, she knows pegasuses are real.

Sydney Hanson was raised in Minnesota alongside numerous pets and brothers. She is the illustrator of the Unicorn Princesses series and the picture books *Next to You, Escargot*, and *A Book for Escargot*, among many others. Sydney lives in Los Angeles.

www.sydwiki.tumblr.com